DISNEY LEARNING

DISNEY
FROZEN

HOW TO BE A SNOW QUEEN

LEADERSHIP WITH ELSA

Mari Schuh

Lerner Pu

For Aubrey, Autumn, Addison, Ella, Lily, and Natalie.
May you become strong, amazing leaders. —MS

Lerner Publications Company
A division of Lerner Publishing Group, Inc.
241 First Avenue North
Minneapolis, MN 55401 USA

For reading levels and more information, look up this title at www.lernerbooks.com

Main body text set in Mikado a 14.5/22.
Typeface provided by HVD Fonts.

Library of Congress Cataloging-in-Publication Data

Names: Schuh, Mari C., 1975- author.
Title: How to be a Snow Queen : leadership with Elsa / Mari Schuh.
Description: Minneapolis : Lerner Publications, [2019] | Series: Disney great character guides | Audience: Age: 6–10. | Audience: K to Grade 3. | Includes bibliographical references.
Identifiers: LCCN 2018019329 (print) | LCCN 2018022739 (ebook) | ISBN 9781541543133 (eb pdf) | ISBN 9781541538993 (lb : alk. paper) | ISBN 9781541546011 (pb : alk. paper)
Subjects: LCSH: Leadership—Juvenile literature.
Classification: LCC HM1261 (ebook) | LCC HM1261 .S368 2019 (print) | DDC 303.3/4—dc23

LC record available at https://lccn.loc.gov/2018019329

Manufactured in the United States of America
1-45082-35909-7/19/2018

Table of Contents

The Right Candidate 4

Growing Up 8

First Day on the Job 14

Facing a Challenge 20

Lessons to Learn 24

All in a Day's Work 30
Glossary 32
To Learn More 32

The Right Candidate

Have you ever dreamed of being a queen? Do you think it would be fun to wear a glittery crown and rule the land? Who wouldn't want that? But being a queen is about more than living in a big castle and throwing fancy parties. Queens must have great leadership skills.

Queens have a big job. It takes just the right candidate to rule a whole kingdom wisely. And just like leaders around the world, Queen Elsa has to take care of a lot of different people. She must also learn to use her magical powers responsibly. So what's it *really* like to have the cool job of snow queen?

Growing Up

A new day is beginning in the kingdom of Arendelle. Inside the castle, Princesses Elsa and Anna are playing. When Elsa grows up, she'll have the important job of queen. But today, she's a young princess having fun with her sister.

Elsa has a secret. She was born with magical powers. She can make snow and ice! Elsa's magic makes her younger sister smile and laugh.

"This is amazing!" Anna says.

Did You Know?

At first, Disney artists thought about making Elsa's hair black and her skin blue!

As they play, Elsa accidentally hits Anna with her magic. Anna is hurt. "I know where we have to go," says their father, the king. The king takes his family to Troll Valley.

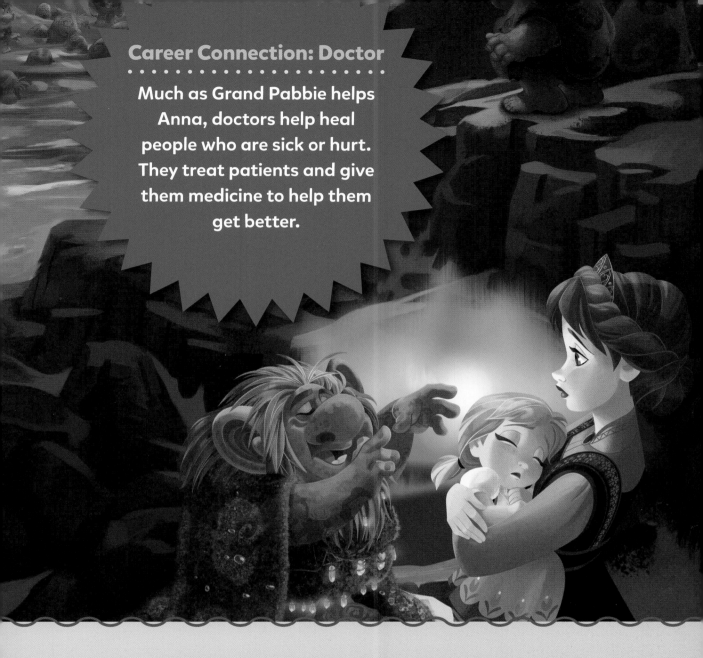

A troll named Grand Pabbie heals Anna. He also takes away Anna's memories of Elsa's magic. Grand Pabbie warns Elsa that her powers will get stronger. "There is beauty in it," he tells her, "but also great danger. You must learn to control it. Fear will be your enemy."

The king still believes Elsa can be a great queen.

The king orders the castle gates closed and reduces the staff. "Keep her powers hidden from everyone," he says, "including Anna."

Elsa needs to work to control her powers. Good leaders try to never harm others. And she can't risk hurting anybody else, especially not Anna. As Elsa grows older, she still isn't sure how to stop her powers. She feels lonely and scared.

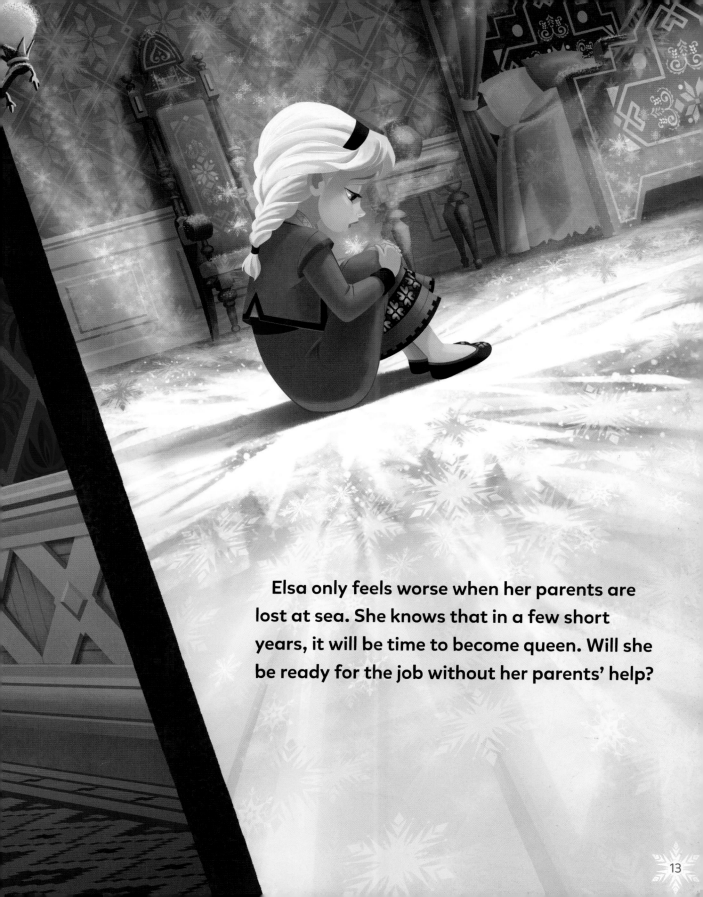

Elsa only feels worse when her parents are lost at sea. She knows that in a few short years, it will be time to become queen. Will she be ready for the job without her parents' help?

First Day on the Job

✳ ✳ ✳

Time passes, and the big day finally arrives. It's Elsa's coronation day! The castle gates open so everyone can celebrate the crowning of their new queen. Elsa is still worried about her powers. But she knows she must step up as queen. Good leaders live up to their responsibilities.

Even though she's afraid, Elsa manages to keep her powers hidden during the coronation.

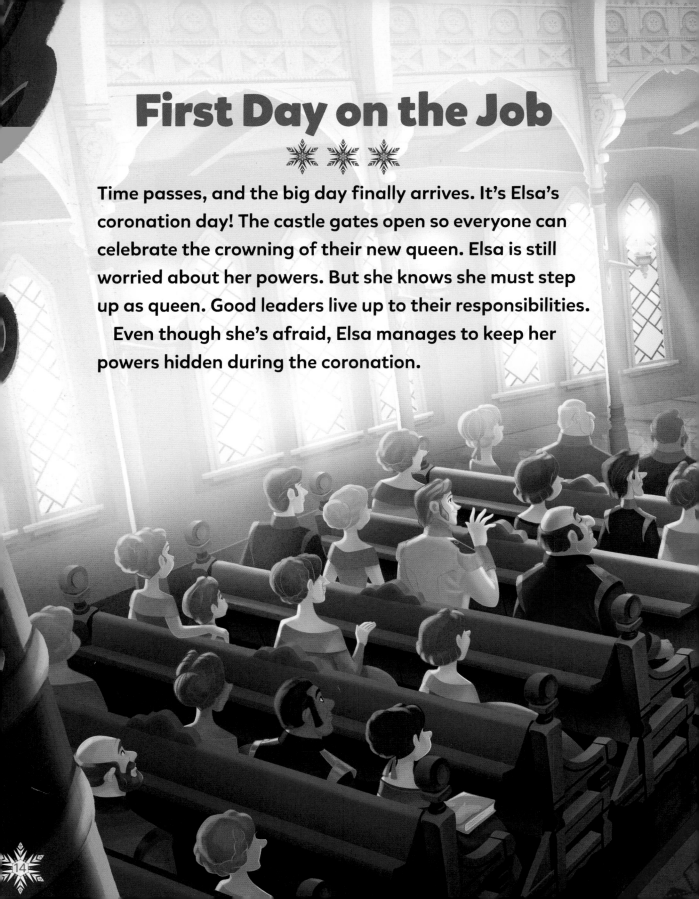

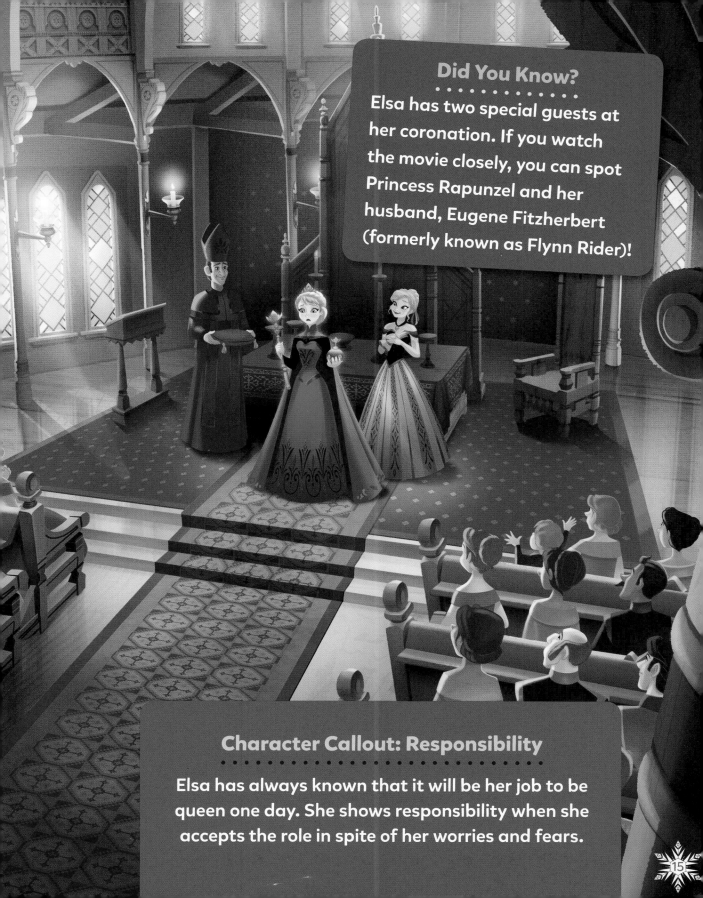

Did You Know?

Elsa has two special guests at her coronation. If you watch the movie closely, you can spot Princess Rapunzel and her husband, Eugene Fitzherbert (formerly known as Flynn Rider)!

Character Callout: Responsibility

Elsa has always known that it will be her job to be queen one day. She shows responsibility when she accepts the role in spite of her worries and fears.

But the day isn't over. At the coronation ball, Anna has news for Elsa. She has met a young prince named Hans, and they would like to get married.

"You can't marry a man you just met," Elsa says. The sisters argue, and Elsa loses control of her powers. She shoots ice across the dance floor. It scares the guests. "Please just stay away from me!" she shouts. As she gets more upset, Elsa's powers get stronger. Everything she touches turns to ice. She runs away to the mountains because she thinks she's not the right person to be queen. But she leaves Arendelle in a snowy, icy winter.

Anna knows Arendelle needs a good leader. And she still believes her sister can do the job. Anna decides to go after Elsa. "I'll bring her back, and I'll make this right," Anna says.

During her search, she meets a man named Kristoff and his reindeer, Sven. She asks Kristoff to help her. She knows it can sometimes take a team of people to get a job done.

Career Connection: Park Ranger

Park rangers protect state and national parks. They protect the plants and animals that live in the parks and the people who visit. Like Kristoff and Anna, park rangers sometimes search for people who are lost or hurt.

Facing a Challenge

Meanwhile, Queen Elsa is alone at the North Mountain. With no one else around, she doesn't have to worry about hiding her magic anymore. Elsa realizes that she can use her powers to make amazing things. She creates a friendly snowman named Olaf and a beautiful palace. She's beginning to believe in herself, just as strong leaders do.

Career Connection: Architect
· · · · · · · ·

Architects help make buildings. It takes creativity to be an architect, just as Elsa is creative with her powers.

Character Callout: Creativity
· ·

When Elsa reaches the North Mountain, she lets her creativity flow. She uses her power to build a huge palace made of ice. Creativity can also help leaders solve problems.

Elsa enjoys being alone in her palace. But suddenly, she hears her sister's voice. Anna has found her ice palace with the help of Kristoff and Olaf. Anna tells Elsa that she's there to take her back to Arendelle, where she belongs.

Elsa disagrees. "I belong here, alone. Where I can be who I am without hurting anybody." She asks her sister to go. "I'm just trying to protect you," she says.

But Anna explains that Elsa needs to return to Arendelle. She has left the kingdom stuck in winter. "But it's OK," Anna says. "You can just unfreeze it."

Elsa is queen, but even the best leaders don't have all the answers. Elsa doesn't know how to unfreeze the kingdom. "I can't," she cries. Elsa loses control of her powers again. An icy blast hits Anna in the heart.

Did You Know?
Elsa's ice palace has six sides, just like a snowflake. The palace changes colors to show how Elsa is feeling. It's blue when she's calm and red when she's afraid.

Lessons to Learn

Anna, Kristoff, and Olaf leave. But Elsa is not alone for long.
Hans and some soldiers appear at her palace. They corner Elsa.
"Stay away," she warns. But the soldiers attack her. They
still think she is a monster. Elsa uses her icy powers to defend
herself. Still, the soldiers capture her and bring the queen back
to Arendelle in chains.

Anna has also returned to Arendelle. She is freezing and needs to find Hans. She thinks his true love is the only thing that can save her. If she doesn't find him soon, her whole body will turn to ice. But Anna learns that she was wrong about Hans. He was just using her to gain control of Arendelle. He is greedy and cruel. He doesn't have what it takes to be a true leader.

Hans locks Anna in a room and goes to find Elsa, who has broken free from her cell. He tells Elsa that her magic has killed her sister. "I tried to save her, but it was too late. Your sister is dead because of you," he lies.

Elsa thinks her worst fear has come true. She has not been a good sister or a good queen. Elsa falls to the ground in grief.

Anna is cold and weak, but she is still alive. With Olaf's help, she escapes the castle. She finds Hans standing over Elsa with a sword.

Anna rushes to save her sister. She throws herself in front of Elsa just as her whole body turns to ice. Her icy hand shatters the sword.

Elsa looks up and sees what Anna has become because of her magic. She cries as she hugs her frozen sister. Suddenly, Anna begins to thaw. Elsa can't believe her eyes! "You sacrificed yourself, for me?" Elsa asks.

"I love you," Anna explains.

Anna's act of true love has thawed her frozen heart and saved her sister. Because of Anna, Elsa knows the power of true love. She has learned that love is more powerful than fear. And that love is the key to her powers. She can become a great leader if she trusts herself, accepts help from others, and uses her skills for the good of Arendelle.

"I never knew what
I was capable of!"

Glossary

architect: a person who designs homes and other buildings as a job

candidate: someone who is seeking a job

confidence: a feeling of trust or belief in yourself or others

coronation: the ceremony during which a king or queen is crowned

kingdom: a country or area that is ruled by a king or queen

meteorology: the study of weather and climate

national park: a large area of land set aside by the government for everyone in the nation to use

To Learn More

Books
Bazaldua, Barbara. *Disney Frozen: The Essential Guide*. New York: DK, 2014.
Relive the movie *Frozen* while learning interesting facts about the movie's characters and locations.

Schuh, Mari. *How to Be King of Pride Rock: Confidence with Simba*.
Minneapolis: Lerner Publications, 2019.
Follow Simba's journey as he grows up and learns the valuable character trait of confidence!

Websites
Disney: *Frozen*
https://frozen.disney.com
Have even more fun with *Frozen* activities. Take a *Frozen* quiz, and enjoy coloring pages, crafts, and scavenger hunts.

Oh My Disney: Quiz—Which *Frozen* Character Are You?
https://ohmy.disney.com/quiz/2014/05/28/quiz-which-frozen-character
-are-you/
Take this quiz to learn which *Frozen* character you are most like.